A FOX, A PIG, AND A DIG

For P, who thought the
sand was snow—JF

PENGUIN WORKSHOP
An imprint of Penguin Random House LLC, New York

First published in the United States of America by Penguin Workshop,
an imprint of Penguin Random House LLC, New York, 2024

Visit us online at penguinrandomhouse.com.

Library of Congress Cataloging-in-Publication Data is available.

Manufactured in China

ISBN 9780593661215 (paperback)   10 9 8 7 6 5 4 3 2 1 TOPL
ISBN 9780593661222 (library binding)   10 9 8 7 6 5 4 3 2 1 TOPL

A FOX, A PIG, AND A DIG

by Jonathan Fenske

Penguin Workshop

PART ONE

9

10

11

But wait!
I do not need to dig.

There is no Fox,
you silly Pig!

So itchy.

That sneaky Fox.
He is so bad!

PART TWO

19

I see a scoop.
I see a box.
I see the sea.
I see a fox.

Hee-hee.

But this pig is not fooled at all.

I know THAT fox is just a doll.

COWABUNGA!

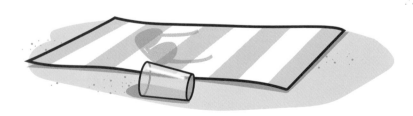

26

28

30

PART THREE

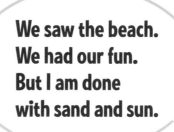